# Just for me, Just for you

*Just for Me, Just for You* is the book with something extra. Each story is specifically crafted to entertain and build preliteracy skills in readers-to-be.

☀ **Wordless stories:** The wordless stories give kids a chance to read to you. Ask your child to use the pictures to tell the story.

☀ **Rhyming stories:** When you see the large type it's your child's turn to chime in with the rhyming words.

☀ **Refrains:** Some stories have refrains in large type. Encourage your child to join in and read the refrains with you!

You'll find that *Just for Me, Just for You* is the perfect book to share together with your little reader!

SIMON & SCHUSTER BOOKS FOR YOUNG READERS
An imprint of Simon & Schuster Children's Publishing Division
1230 Avenue of the Americas, New York, New York 10020

Book design by Felicity Erwin and Dan Potash
Manufactured in China
10 9 8 7 6 5 4 3 2 1
Cataloging-in-Publication Data is available from the Library of Congress.
ISBN 0-689-85963-5

Special thanks to the Nick Jr. family of children's writers and illustrators and the entire
*Nick Jr. Family Magazine* team who made this book possible including:
Dan Sullivan, Senior Vice President; Freddi Greenberg, Editor in Chief; Don Morris, Design Director;
Susan Hood, Special Projects Editor; Sherri Lerner, Managing Editor; Hally Burak, Publishing Planning Director

# Just for me, Just for you

Introduction by Freddi Greenberg, Editor in Chief
*Nick Jr. Family Magazine*

## Simon & Schuster Books for Young Readers

New York    London    Toronto    Sydney    Singapore

# Contents

# Introduction

Every family has its own good-night ritual. For our kids the part that was non-negotiable was the bedtime story. Between toothbrushing and lights out, my kids heard the names Margaret Wise Brown and Eric Carle so often, they actually thought they were friends of the family.

Besides the cuddling and comfort that come with story time, kids get so much more out of books than just words and pictures. *Nick Jr. Family Magazine* Read-Together Stories actually give kids a part to play and say. These special stories help build ready-to-read skills. The wordless stories are for the youngest child. Ask your pre-reader to look at the pictures and tell you the story of "The Great Escape" or "Peekaboo Moon." Encouraging children to be storytellers introduces them to the basics: All stories have a beginning, a middle, and an end. Other stories like "All Aboard!" use repeating words that kids will soon learn to recognize on sight. "The Best-Dressed Guest" invites kids to look, listen, and finish a rhyme. When children begin to look forward to a refrain or fill in a rhyme, they get practice in word and sound recognition and the confidence that comes with feeling like a reader, even if they're not quite there yet.

At *Nick Jr. Family Magazine* we're all about being together. The Read-Together Stories in this book were created for us by today's most renowned children's book authors and illustrators, such as Jack Prelutsky and Chris Raschka. When these stories first appeared in our magazine, we discovered that grown-ups like them as much as kids do! I have a feeling that once you've read them a couple of hundred times with your kids, your kids will think we're friends of the family too.

Sweet dreams!

*Freddi Greenberg*

Freddi Greenberg
Editor in Chief

NICK JR
*family magazine*

# Hello, My Little Friend

By Andrea Perry
Illustrated by Ward Schumaker

The ladybug has tiny spots,
reminding me of polka dots.

## Hello, my little friend!

Spider's ready to begin.

He has a silky web to spin.

## Hello, my little friend!

Butterflies and bumblebees
seem to float along the breeze.

Hello, my little friend!

8

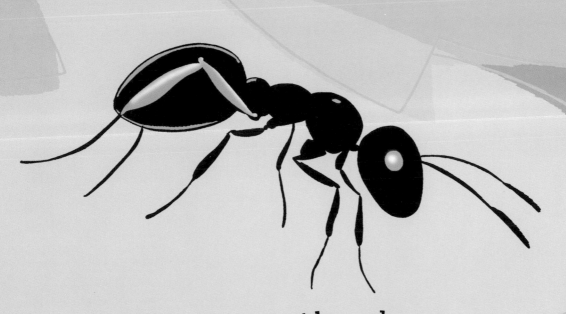

If you look beneath a plant,
chances are you'll see an ant.

# Hello, my little friend!

The cricket chirps from in a tree.
Could he be calling out to me?

# Hello, my little friend!

**The End**

# Look Who's Here!

By Catherine Lukas
Illustrated by Scott Nash

Ding-Dong! went the doorbell chime.
"He's here!" yelled Tom. "And right on time.
I made the coolest friend today."
Tom beamed at Mom, "He's come to play!"

11

"He says he'd like to play outside."

16

# THE GREAT ESCAPE

By Tracey Keevan
Illustrated by
Robert Van Nutt

**2**

**1**

**5**

**6**

THE END

# It's HOT, HOT, HOT!

By Michaela Muntean
Illustrated by Chris Raschka

Summer sunshine beats on sizzling city streets. There's no need to wear a lot.... It's HOT, HOT, HOT!

Summer sunshine heats
sunflowers, berries, beets.
The plants all say,
forget-me-not.

# It's HOT, HOT, HOT!

Summer sunshine meets
the sea in gold-streaked sheets.
Find yourself a shady spot....

It's HOT, HOT, HOT!

Icy treats on sticks to lick,
sprinklers spinning—run through quick!
Or jump into a swimming pool....

# Don't Wake the Baby!

By Sarah Albee

Illustrated by
Marjory Wunsch

1

4

5

2

3

The End

# All Aboard!

BY KAREN BAICKER
ILLUSTRATED BY ROBERT VAN NUTT

Jake loves trains and that's a fact—
the kind that whistle 'round the track.
*Chug-a-lug-a-clickity-clack!*

## All aboard!

Without his trains, Jake can pretend
and line his shoes up 'round the bend.
His boot caboose brings up the end.

## All aboard!

"Toot Toot Whoo Whoo,
Chattanooga Choo Choo.
Pufferbelly, comin' through!"

All aboard!

Conductor Jake is never far.
He's snacking in the dining car
and floating in the bathing car.

All aboard!

Chicago, Boston, Baltimore,
It's final call on Platform Four.
Stand clear and watch the closing door.

All aboard!

The engine gets the signal light.
The train is speeding out of sight.
Jake throws the switch and says good night!

All aboard!

The End

# "WHERE'S MY SHOE?"

By Jean Marzollo • Illustrated by Martin Matje

Where, oh, where is my other shoe?
I only have one.
Where is number two?

Spangly silver
high-heeled shoe—
for Mommy, it's fine,

but it's
not mine.

Shiny black
lace-up shoe—
for Daddy, it's fine,

**but it's
not mine.**

40

Ride-'em-cowboy
leather boot—
for brother, it's fine,

**but it's
not mine.**

Short red
garden clog—
for Grandma, it's fine,

**but it's
not mine.**

Knee-high green
fishing boot—
for Grandpa, it's fine,

**but it's
not mine.**

43

High-top sneaker
with one blue star—
for me, that's fine;

it's mine,
mine, mine!

The End

By Tish Rabe
Illustrated by Lydia Monks

# The Best-Dressed Guest

It's party time, and we're invited!
All our friends are so excited—

spiders hanging upside down,
a princess with a crooked **crown.**

The strangest guests you've ever seen.
Do you know why? It's **Halloween!**

45

Then suddenly the door goes *boom*!
A little ghost begins to zoom
and zig and zag around the room
and trips over the witch's **broom!**

"I'll stop him!"
cries Old Mother Goose.
"I'll stop him!"
cries the box of **juice.**

"I'll stop him!" cries the circus **clown,**
whose cupcake landed upside down.

48

"I'll stop him!"
cries the orange bug,
who runs to give
the ghost a **hug.**

49

But falling down around his feet
is nothing but an empty **sheet!**

The princess laughs. "Oh, this is funny!
That's no ghost! It's our pet . . . **bunny!**"

**The End**

**The End**

By Jack Prelutsky
Illustrated by Olivier Dunrea

# Here Comes Snow!

Winter's putting on a show.
**Here comes snow. Here comes snow.**

Icy breezes blow and blow.

Here comes snow. Here comes snow.

Cheeks are red and noses glow.
**Here comes snow. Here comes snow.**

Bundle up and come outside.
You will find me, I won't hide.

I'm a snowman. Help me grow.
# Here comes snow. Here comes snow.

**The End**

# Peekaboo Moon

By Susan Hood
Illustrated by Mercedes MacDonald

2

3

6 ▶

The End

# Nick Jr.
## FamilyMagazine

### Order today and receive
### 10 Issues for just $1.99* an issue

Featuring Blue's Clues and all your favorite Nick Jr. characters, this magazine is filled with do-together activities and stories for parents and their young children to share. In just 10 minutes, it will provide hours of learning and entertainment for any family. Nick Jr. Magazine... It's where kids play to learn and parents learn to play.

Send to:
Name _____

Address _____

City _____ State _____ Zip _____

Bill to:
Name _____

Address _____

City _____ State _____ Zip _____
Please enter your e-mail address to receive subscription information, special offers, and news from Nickelodeon or its partners.

Parent's e-mail address _____

☐ Payment Enclosed
☐ Bill Me
(circle one)
☐ Charge My VISA / MASTERCARD

Credit Card # _____

Exp. Date _____

Signature _____

KSIMONS1
10/2290

© 2003 Viacom International Inc. All rights reserved. Nick Jr. and all related titles, logos, and characters are trademarks of Viacom International Inc. Nick Jr. publishes 8 issues per year, bimonthly, except monthly in August, September, October and November. Please allow 6-8 weeks for delivery. Canadian orders: $32.90 U.S.$ (includes 7% GST). Foreign orders: $33.90 U.S.$. *Plus U.S. postage and handling of .30¢ an issue. Offer expires 6/30/04.

---

# Nick Jr.
## FamilyMagazine

### Order today and receive
### 10 Issues for just $1.99* an issue

Featuring Blue's Clues and all your favorite Nick Jr. characters, this magazine is filled with do-together activities and stories for parents and their young children to share. In just 10 minutes, it will provide hours of learning and entertainment for any family. Nick Jr. Magazine... It's where kids play to learn and parents learn to play.

Send to:
Name _____

Address _____

City _____ State _____ Zip _____

Bill to:
Name _____

Address _____

City _____ State _____ Zip _____
Please enter your e-mail address to receive subscription information, special offers, and news from Nickelodeon or its partners.

Parent's e-mail address _____

☐ Payment Enclosed
☐ Bill Me
(circle one)
☐ Charge My VISA / MASTERCARD

Credit Card # _____

Exp. Date _____

Signature _____

KSIMONS2
10/2290

© 2003 Viacom International Inc. All rights reserved. Nick Jr. and all related titles, logos, and characters are trademarks of Viacom International Inc. Nick Jr. publishes 8 issues per year, bimonthly, except monthly in August, September, October and November. Please allow 6-8 weeks for delivery. Canadian orders: $32.90 U.S.$ (includes 7% GST). Foreign orders: $33.90 U.S.$. *Plus U.S. postage and handling of .30¢ an issue. Offer expires 6/30/04.

---

# NICKELODEON MAGAZINE

This award-winning entertainment and humor magazine for kids is packed with fascinating facts, celebrity interviews, comics, pull-outs, puzzles, activities, and the inside scoop on Nick TV.

### 12 Issues for $1.99* an Issue!
☐ Payment Enclosed  ☐ Bill Me  ☐ Visa/Mastercard
(circle one)

Send To: Name _____

Address _____

City _____ State _____ Zip _____

Bill To: Name _____

Address _____

City _____ State _____ Zip _____
Please enter your e-mail address to receive subscription information, special offers, and news from Nickelodeon or its partners.

Parent's e-mail address _____

Credit Card # _____

Exp. Date _____

Signature _____

12/2748
KSIMONS3

© 2003 Viacom International Inc. All Rights Reserved. Nickelodeon, and all related characters are trademarks of Viacom International Inc. Nickelodeon publishes 10 issues a year, monthly except for January and July. Combined, expanded, and premium issues count as two subscription issues. Please allow 6-8 weeks for delivery. SpongeBob SquarePants created by Stephen Hillenburg. Offer expires 6/30/04. *Plus 30¢ US postage and handling per issue. Canadian orders: $39.48 US$ (include 7% GST). Foreign orders: $40.48 US$.

## BUSINESS REPLY MAIL
FIRST-CLASS MAIL    PERMIT NO. 8555    DES MOINES IA

POSTAGE WILL BE PAID BY ADDRESSEE

Nick Jr. Magazine
P.O. BOX 3234
Harlan IA 51593-2414

Thanks for
your order!

---

## BUSINESS REPLY MAIL
FIRST-CLASS MAIL    PERMIT NO. 8555    DES MOINES IA

POSTAGE WILL BE PAID BY ADDRESSEE

Nick Jr. Magazine
P.O. BOX 3234
Harlan IA 51593-2414

Thanks for
your order!

---

## BUSINESS REPLY MAIL
FIRST-CLASS MAIL    PERMIT NO. 8555    DES MOINES IA

POSTAGE WILL BE PAID BY ADDRESSEE

**NICKELODEON MAGAZINE**
**P.O. BOX 3235**
**HARLAN IA 51593-2415**

**Thanks for
your order!**